SUMMER CAMP
SCIENCE
MYSTERIES

#7 The Great
Space Case

A Mystery
about Astronomy

by Lynda Beauregard

illustrated by Der-shing Helmer

GRAPHIC UNIVERSE™ • MINNEAPOLIS

Angie Rayez

Alex Rayez

Jordan Collins

Braelin Walker

Megan Taylor

Carly Livingston

DON'T MISS THE EXPERIMENTS ON PAGES 45 AND 46!

Kyle Reed

Loraine Sanders

MYSTERIOUS WORDS AND MORE ON PAGE 47!

J. D. Hamilton

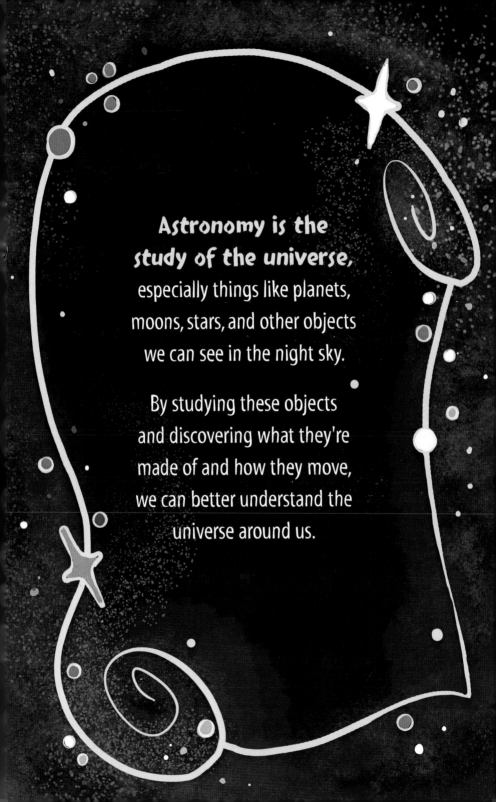

**Astronomy is the study of the universe,** especially things like planets, moons, stars, and other objects we can see in the night sky.

By studying these objects and discovering what they're made of and how they move, we can better understand the universe around us.

Story by Lynda Beauregard

Art by Der-shing Helmer

Coloring by Jenn Manley Lee

Lettering by Grace Lu

Graphic Universe™
A division of Lerner Publishing Group, Inc.
241 First Avenue North
Minneapolis, MN 55401 U.S.A.

Website address: www.lernerbooks.com

Main body text set in CCWildwords.
Typeface provided by Comicraft/Active Images.

Library of Congress Cataloging-in-Publication Data

Beauregard, Lynda, author.
    The great space case : a mystery about astronomy / by Lynda Beauregard ;
illustrated by Der-shing Helmer.
        pages    cm. — (Summer camp science mysteries ; #7)
        ISBN 978–1–4677–0169–3 (library binding : alk. paper)
        1. Astronomy—Experiments—Juvenile literature. I. Helmer, Der-shing,
illustrator. II. Title.
QB46.B378  2013
741.5'973—dc23                                    2012023871

Manufactured in the United States of America
2 - 45454 - 12759 - 11/12/2018

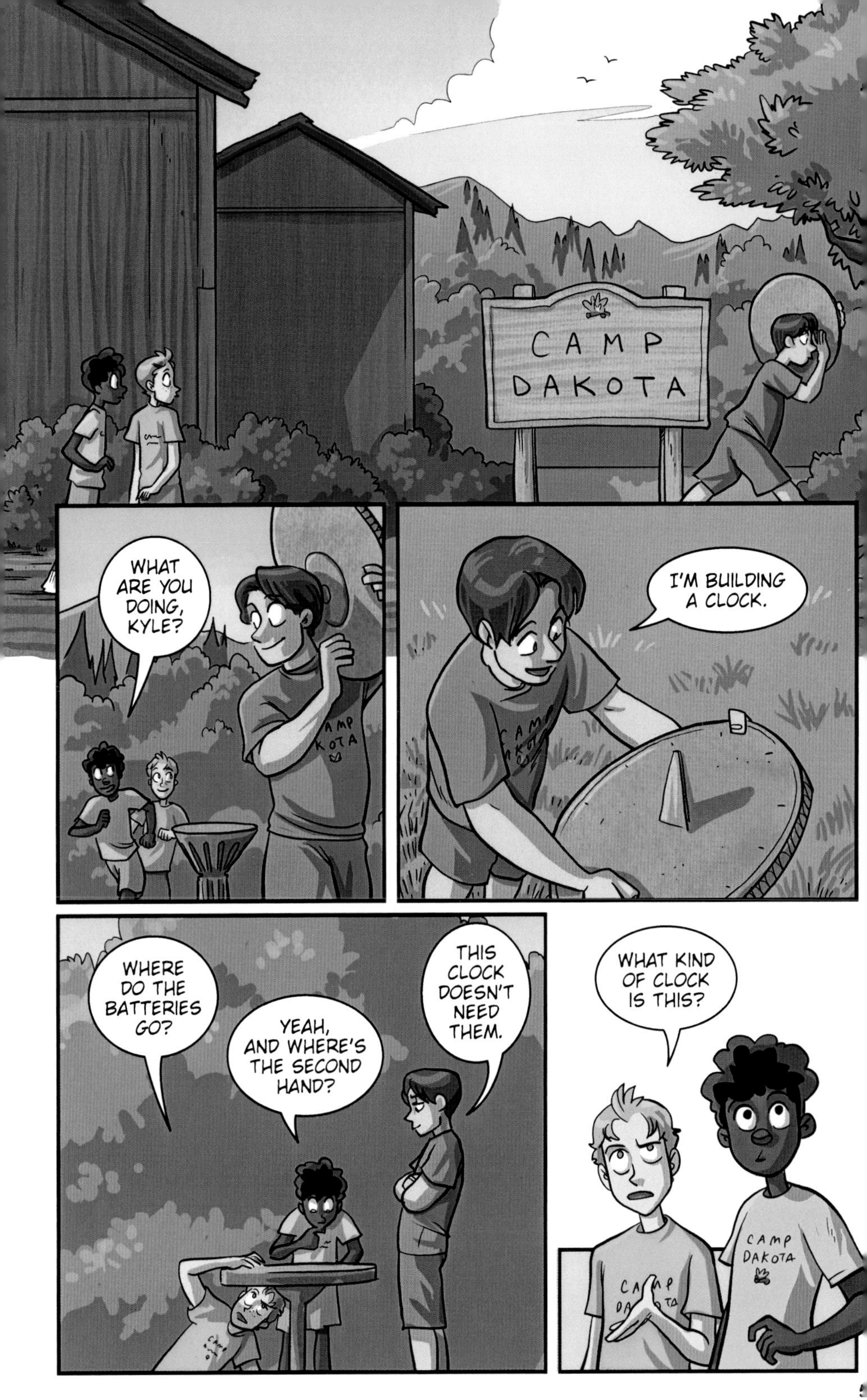
CAMP
DAKOTA
WHAT ARE YOU DOING, KYLE?
I'M BUILDING A CLOCK.
WHERE DO THE BATTERIES GO?
YEAH, AND WHERE'S THE SECOND HAND?
THIS CLOCK DOESN'T NEED THEM.
WHAT KIND OF CLOCK IS THIS?
CAMP DAKOTA

IT'S A SUNDIAL! IT USES THE SUN TO TELL YOU WHAT TIME IT IS.

CAMP DAKOTA

THE SUN HITS THIS POINTER, CALLED A GNOMON, AND CREATES A SHADOW.

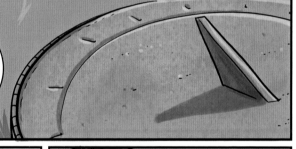

THE SHADOW POINTS TO THE MARKINGS ON THE FACE. AND SINCE FROM OUR POINT OF VIEW THE SUN IS ALWAYS MOVING, THE SHADOW KEEPS MOVING TOO.

SO WHAT HAPPENS AT NIGHT?

OR ON CLOUDY DAYS?

CAMP DAKOTA

CAMP DAKOTA

CAMP DAKOTA

SUNDIALS DON'T WORK VERY WELL THEN!

I THINK I'LL JUST STICK TO USING MY WATCH.

WHAT'S GOING ON OVER THERE?

I THINK IT'S TIME FOR LORAINE'S BIG ANNOUNCEMENT. LET'S JOIN THEM.

LISTEN UP, EVERYBODY! IT'S SPACE WEEK!

WE'VE GOT A FEW THINGS PLANNED, AND THERE'S A *BIG* EVENT HAPPENING IN A FEW DAYS THAT I'M VERY EXCITED ABOUT.

BUT RIGHT NOW, I WANT TO TALK ABOUT A COMPETITION!

I WANT YOU ALL TO BREAK UP INTO TEAMS OF FOUR.

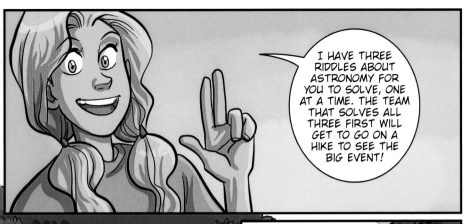

I HAVE THREE RIDDLES ABOUT ASTRONOMY FOR YOU TO SOLVE, ONE AT A TIME. THE TEAM THAT SOLVES ALL THREE FIRST WILL GET TO GO ON A HIKE TO SEE THE BIG EVENT!

SO GET YOUR TEAMS TOGETHER AND THINK UP A COOL TEAM NAME. I'LL GIVE YOU YOUR FIRST RIDDLE AFTER DINNER.

THIS IS GREAT! I TOTALLY ROCK AT ASTRONOMY. IT'S MY FAVORITE SUBJECT!

OK, LET'S BE A TEAM!

WHAT ABOUT ME?

OH NO! WE CAN ONLY HAVE FOUR, BRAELIN.

YOU CAN BE ON OUR TEAM, I GUESS. WE NEED ONE MORE PERSON.

WHO ELSE IS ON THE TEAM?

LUKE AND CLIFF. LUKE IS MY NEW BOYFRIEND, AND CLIFF IS HIS ROOMIE.

YUCK!

YOU'RE ON THE RIGHT TEAM, BUDDY. THOSE KIDS WON'T BE ANY GOOD AT SCIENCE STUFF.

I DON'T KNOW ABOUT THAT...

OR MAYBE JUST THE PARTS OF IT WE CAN SEE...

SO LET'S START OFF SPACE WEEK WITH A BIG SUBJECT-- THE GALAXY!

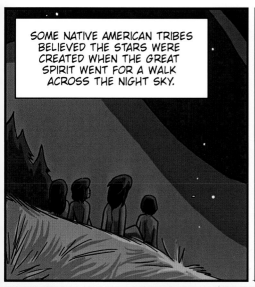

SOME NATIVE AMERICAN TRIBES BELIEVED THE STARS WERE CREATED WHEN THE GREAT SPIRIT WENT FOR A WALK ACROSS THE NIGHT SKY.

HIS WALKING STICK POKED HOLES IN THE SKY, LETTING LIGHT SHINE THROUGH. THIS MADE THE STARS.

REALLY?

THAT'S **NOT** HOW STARS ARE MADE.

WE KNOW THAT NOW! BUT WE STILL TELL STORIES ABOUT THE STARS, DON'T WE?

LIKE THE CONSTELLATIONS?

EXACTLY! WHEN WE LOOK AT THE STARS, WE DRAW LINES BETWEEN THEM, MAKING IMAGES, AND GIVE THEM NAMES. WE USE THE NAMES THAT THE ANCIENT GREEKS CAME UP WITH, BUT OTHER PEOPLE GAVE THEM NAMES TOO.

FOR INSTANCE, DOES EVERYBODY KNOW WHAT THIS IS?

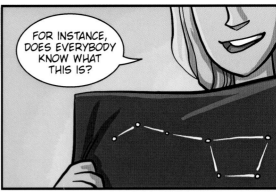

THE BIG DIPPER!

RIGHT! BUT WHEN THE GERMANS LOOKED AT THESE STARS, THEY SAW A WAGON.

THE ANCIENT BRITONS THOUGHT IT WAS KING ARTHUR, RIDING IN HIS CHARIOT.

AND THE SEMINOLE TRIBE THOUGHT IT WAS A BIG BOAT THAT CARRIED GOOD SOULS TO THEIR FINAL RESTING PLACE.

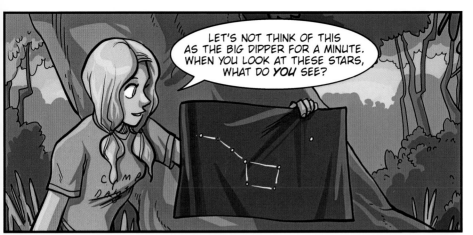

LET'S NOT THINK OF THIS AS THE BIG DIPPER FOR A MINUTE. WHEN YOU LOOK AT THESE STARS, WHAT DO *YOU* SEE?

I SEE A ROLLER COASTER.

I SEE MY DAD RELAXING IN HIS LAWN CHAIR.

I SEE A FROG JUMPING ACROSS A POND!

I CAN SEE THAT TOO!

WE CAN ALSO USE THE BIG DIPPER TO FIND POLARIS, THE NORTH STAR. YOU START BY FINDING THE TWO STARS ON THE RIGHT SIDE OF THE BIG DIPPER.

IF WE DRAW A LINE UP THROUGH THOSE STARS, IT TAKES US RIGHT TO POLARIS.

DOES ANYONE KNOW WHY POLARIS IS IMPORTANT?

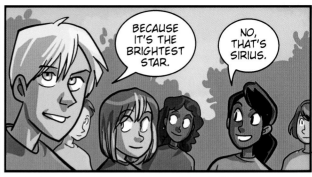

BECAUSE IT'S THE BRIGHTEST STAR.

NO, THAT'S SIRIUS.

THAT'S RIGHT-- SIRIUS IS THE BRIGHTEST, ANGIE. BUT WHAT'S SPECIAL ABOUT POLARIS?

IT'S THE ONLY STAR THAT STAYS WHERE IT'S AT. ALL THE OTHERS MOVE AROUND WITH THE SEASONS.

TECHNICALLY, IT'S EARTH THAT'S MOVING, BUT YOU HAVE THE RIGHT IDEA.

Earth's axis is an imaginary line that runs from the South Pole to the North Pole, and the northern part of this line points almost directly at Polaris. As Earth rotates on its axis, Polaris seems to stay in the same place, while the other stars look as if they're rotating around it.

TO PLAY THE GAME, YOU'LL NEED THIS STAR CHART. BUT FIRST, LET'S EAT DINNER!

WOW, ANGIE, YOU REALLY ARE GOOD AT ALL THIS SPACE STUFF.

YEAH, I *LOVE* GOING TO THE PLANETARIUM.

HEY, WE HAVEN'T COME UP WITH A NAME FOR OUR TEAM YET.

HOW ABOUT STAR TROOPERS?

THAT SOUNDS LIKE THE NAME OF A MOVIE.

HOW ABOUT... ASTRO... SOMETHING...

YEAH...

HOW ABOUT STARRY DREAMS?

BLECH!

LORAINE! WE FIGURED OUT OUR TEAM NAME!

WE'RE THE ASTRO EXPLORERS!

AND WE ARE THE STAR TROOPERS!

...

YOU CAN'T REALLY USE ME IN A SNOWBALL FIGHT. SOMETIMES I FOLLOW MY TAIL. SOMETIMES IT FOLLOWS ME.

WHO IS READY FOR THE FIRST RIDDLE?

WHAT DO YOU THINK, ANGIE?

I DON'T KNOW. I WAS THINKING MAYBE IT HAD TO DO WITH SIRIUS IN CANIS MAJOR, THE BIG DOG CONSTELLATION, BECAUSE OF THE TAIL.

BUT THE TAIL IS ALWAYS BEHIND IT.

THERE ARE OTHER ANIMAL CONSTELLATIONS THAT HAVE TAILS. LIKE MAYBE THE PEGASUS OR THE DRAGON?

NO, THEIR TAILS DON'T MOVE, EITHER. C'MON, LET'S SLEEP ON IT.

THE NEXT MORNING...

ANGIE, WAKE UP!

MMPF.

I COULDN'T SLEEP LAST NIGHT. I KEPT THINKING ABOUT THAT RIDDLE.

MY TEAM CAN'T MAKE ANY SENSE OUT OF IT, EITHER.

HEY, YOU CAN'T SIT HERE!

YEAH, YOU'RE THE ENEMY NOW!

FINE.

I WAS THINKING, IT DOESN'T HAVE TO BE A CONSTELLATION, DOES IT?

I SUPPOSE IT COULD BE SOMETHING ELSE...

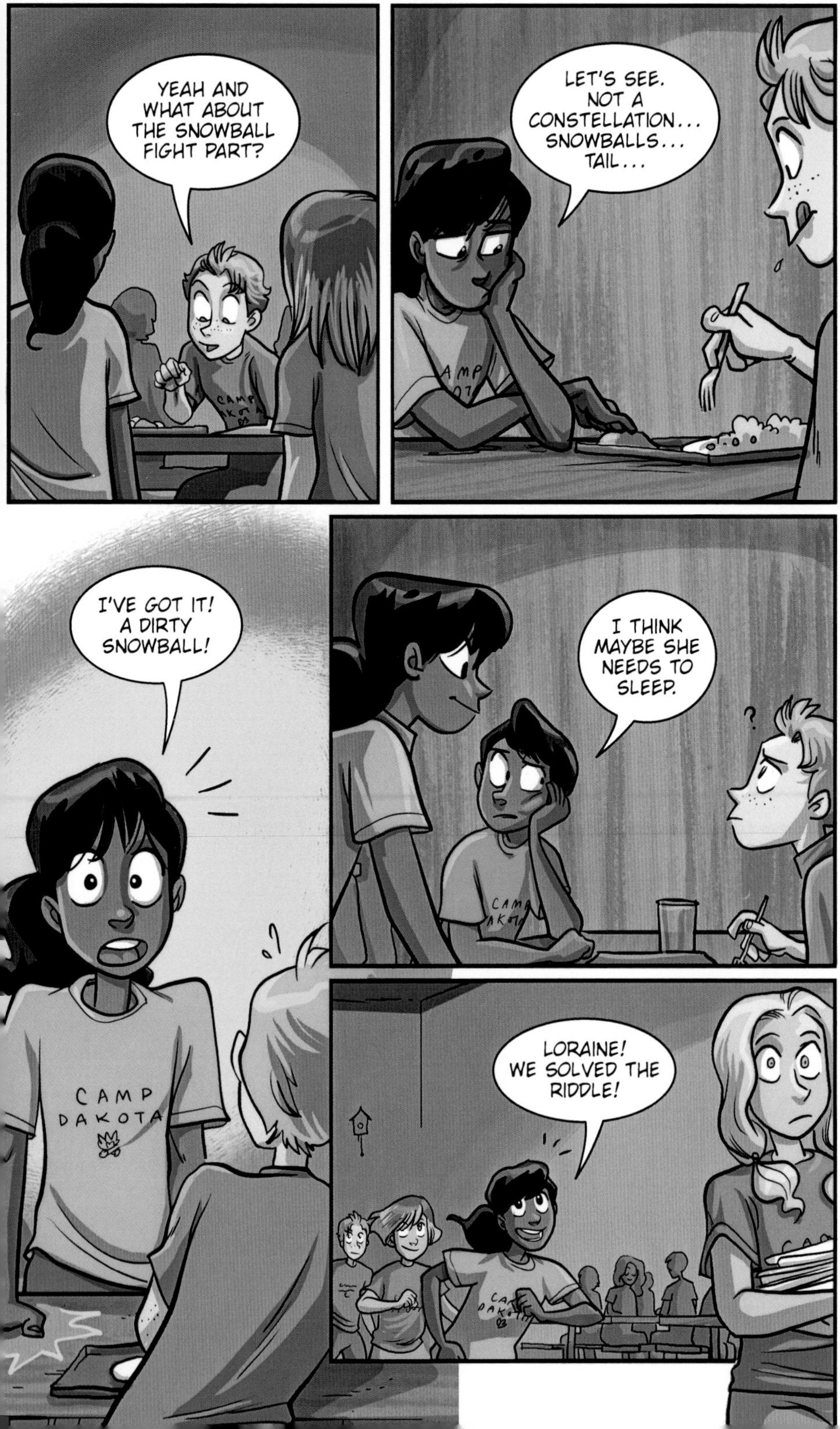
YEAH AND WHAT ABOUT THE SNOWBALL FIGHT PART?
LET'S SEE. NOT A CONSTELLATION... SNOWBALLS... TAIL...
I'VE GOT IT! A DIRTY SNOWBALL!
CAMP DAKOTA
I THINK MAYBE SHE NEEDS TO SLEEP.
LORAINE! WE SOLVED THE RIDDLE!

OK, WHAT IS IT?

IT'S A COMET! IT'S A BIG, DIRTY SNOWBALL, AND ITS TAIL CAN BE IN FRONT OR BEHIND.

Comets are made of ice, rock, and gases. As a comet approaches the Sun, the ice starts to vaporize and forms a tail behind it. But when the comet turns away from the Sun, the solar winds keep the tail in front of it.

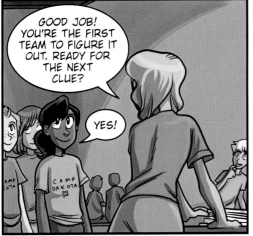

GOOD JOB! YOU'RE THE FIRST TEAM TO FIGURE IT OUT. READY FOR THE NEXT CLUE?

YES!

DON'T MAKE A WISH, BECAUSE I'M NOT WHAT YOU THINK I AM.

THAT'S EVEN WORSE THAN THE FIRST ONE!

GOOD JOB, ASTRO EXPLORERS! ANGIE, YOU DESERVE A NAP.

~:YAWN!:~

HEY, LORAINE, OUR TEAM HAS THE ANSWER TO YOUR RIDDLE.

WE DO?

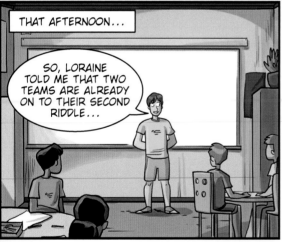

THAT AFTERNOON...

SO, LORAINE TOLD ME THAT TWO TEAMS ARE ALREADY ON TO THEIR SECOND RIDDLE...

TEAM ASTRO EXPLORERS AND TEAM STAR TROOPERS!

WHOO WHOO WHOO

BUT WE DON'T HAVE TIME FOR RIDDLES RIGHT NOW. WE'RE GOING TO THE MOON!

REALLY?!

WELL NO, NOT EXACTLY. YOUR PARENTS PROBABLY WOULDN'T GIVE US PERMISSION FOR THAT.

BUT WE CAN GO THERE USING OUR IMAGINATION!

PRETEND YOU ARE BUILDING A PERMANENT BASE ON THE MOON.

WHAT WILL YOU NEED? WHAT DOES YOUR BASE LOOK LIKE?

WHAT'S THIS OVER HERE?

THAT'S MY FLOWER GARDEN.

OK, LET'S THINK ABOUT THIS. THE MOON HAS SOIL AND LIGHT. WHAT ELSE WOULD FLOWERS NEED?

WATER AND--

--AIR.

RIGHT. THE MOON DOESN'T HAVE ENOUGH GRAVITY TO HOLD ONTO AN ATMOSPHERE, SO AIR IS A PROBLEM.

AND THERE ISN'T ANY WATER ON THE MOON.

WE THINK THERE MIGHT BE SOME IN THE POLAR REGIONS BUT, MOSTLY, NO.

FINE. THESE ARE SPECIAL FLOWERS THAT DON'T NEED AIR OR WATER.

I'LL INVENT THEM!

AND WHAT CAN YOU TELL ME ABOUT YOURS, BRAELIN?

WELL, HERE'S WHERE I'LL SLEEP, HERE'S WHERE I'LL PLAY VIDEO GAMES AND STUFF, AND THIS ROOM IS FOR EATING!

AND WHERE IS YOUR FOOD GOING TO COME FROM?

CAMP DAKOTA

I'LL... HAVE PIZZA DELIVERED EVERY DAY!

DELIVERY BY ROCKET EVERY DAY WOULD BE PRETTY EXPENSIVE. ARE YOU A BILLIONAIRE?

MAYBE I AM!

ALL RIGHT, EVERYONE, LET'S FINISH UP.

I WANT TO TALK ABOUT MY NEW WEIGHT LOSS PLAN.

CAMP DAKOTA

HUH?

NO DIETING, NO EXERCISING, JUST...A TRIP TO THE MOON!

THE GRAVITY ON THE MOON IS ONLY 16.7% OF EARTH'S GRAVITY. TO CHANGE THAT TO A DECIMAL, WE MOVE THE DECIMAL POINT TWO PLACES TO THE LEFT.

16.7

SO IF YOU MULTIPLY YOUR WEIGHT BY .167, YOU'LL FIND OUT HOW MUCH YOU WOULD WEIGH ON THE MOON.

.167 × weight on Earth
= weight on the Moon

UM...I DON'T KNOW HOW TO MULTIPLY DECIMALS YET.

I DO!

WOW, BRAELIN! YOU WOULD WEIGH LESS THAN 14 POUNDS!

.167
× 80
000
13 36
13.36

AND WITHOUT ALL THAT TROUBLESOME GRAVITY, YOU COULD JUMP SIX TIMES AS HIGH!

CAMP DAKOTA

24

EVERYBODY FIND A PARTNER, GRAB A PIECE OF CHALK AND A RULER, AND STAND NEXT TO A WALL.

FIRST, USE THE CHALK TO MARK ON THE WALL HOW TALL YOUR PARTNER IS.

THEN TAKE TURNS JUMPING, AND HAVE YOUR PARTNER MARK HOW HIGH YOUR HEAD REACHED ON THE WALL.

NOW MEASURE HOW HIGH YOU JUMPED.

MULTIPLY THOSE NUMBERS BY 6, AND YOU'LL GET HOW HIGH YOU WOULD BE ABLE TO JUMP ON THE MOON.

LET'S SEE, 18 INCHES... TIMES 6 IS... 108 INCHES!

YOU WOULD HAVE AN AWESOME JUMP SHOT!

HEY, WHY IS EVERYONE HANGING AROUND INSIDE ON A BEAUTIFUL DAY LIKE TODAY?

LET'S TAKE THE CANOES OUT ON THE WATER.

YEAH!

LET'S GO!

HMM... DON'T MAKE A WISH, BECAUSE I'M NOT WHAT YOU THINK I AM...

WHAT'S IT MEAN?

THERE'S... OOF... WISHING WELLS...

AND WISHBONES.

HMM.

WHAT ABOUT... WISHING ON A FALLING STAR?

THAT'S IT!

BUT WHAT ABOUT THE SECOND PART-- I'M NOT WHAT YOU THINK I AM?

A SHOOTING STAR ISN'T A STAR AT ALL. IT'S A METEOR!

Sometimes objects from space, like rocks or metal, enter Earth's atmosphere. The objects move so fast through the air that they start to burn. This forms a streak of light called a meteor.

WHOO! WE FIGURED IT OUT!

YES! LET'S GO FIND LORAINE AND GIVE HER THE ANSWER.

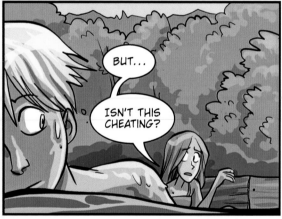

BUT...

ISN'T THIS CHEATING?

CANNONBALL!

EEK! BRAELIN!

LORAINE DIDN'T SAY HOW TO GET THE ANSWER. SHE JUST SAID THE FIRST TEAM TO ANSWER THEM ALL WINS.

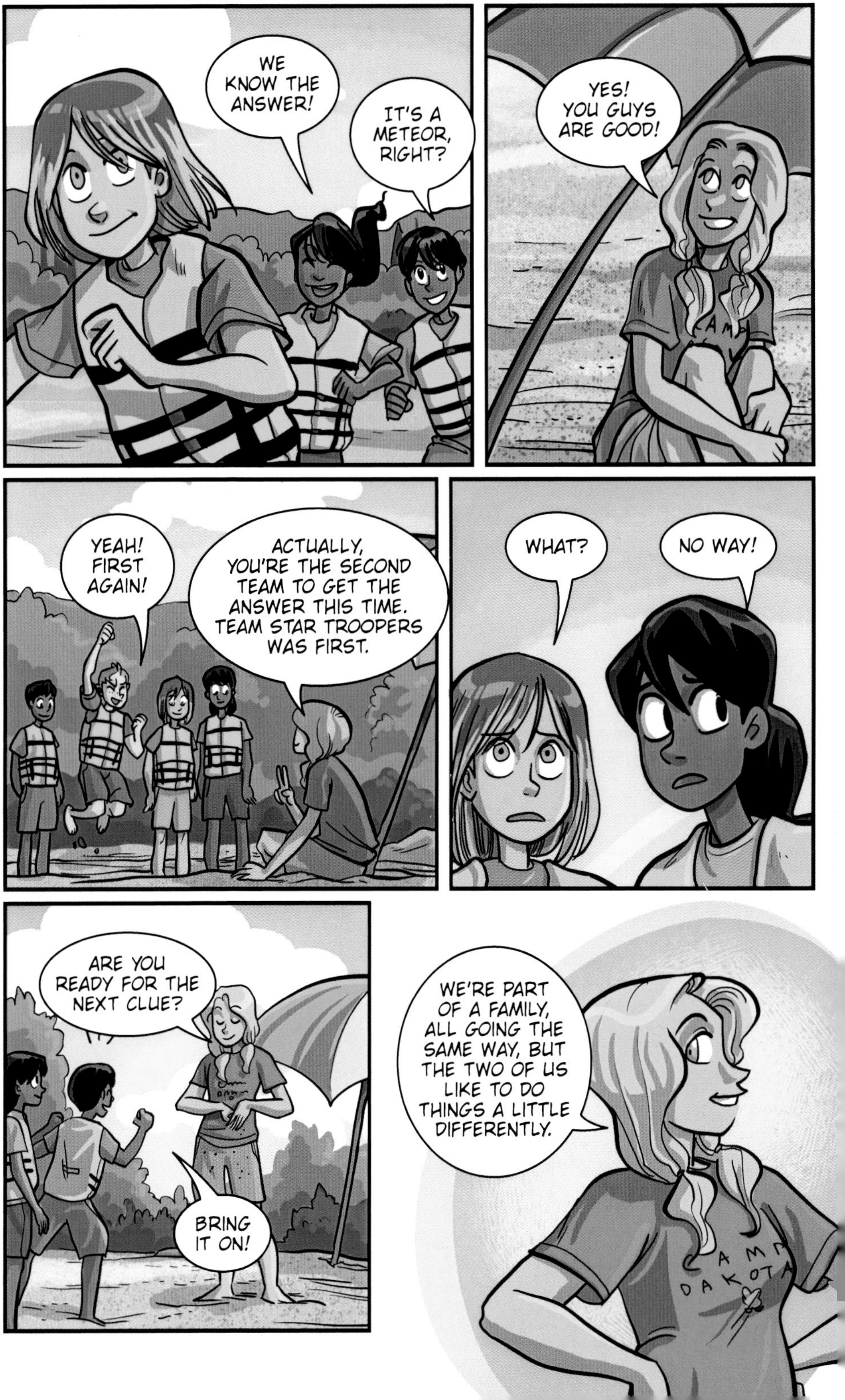
WE KNOW THE ANSWER!
IT'S A METEOR, RIGHT?
YES! YOU GUYS ARE GOOD!
YEAH! FIRST AGAIN!
ACTUALLY, YOU'RE THE SECOND TEAM TO GET THE ANSWER THIS TIME. TEAM STAR TROOPERS WAS FIRST.
WHAT?
NO WAY!
ARE YOU READY FOR THE NEXT CLUE?
BRING IT ON!
WE'RE PART OF A FAMILY, ALL GOING THE SAME WAY, BUT THE TWO OF US LIKE TO DO THINGS A LITTLE DIFFERENTLY.
CAMP DAKOTA

THAT SOUNDS FAMILIAR.

SINCE THE TWO OF US--

--LIKE TO DO THINGS--

--OUR OWN WAY!

HA HA HA!

PART OF A FAMILY...

JUST RELAX. DON'T STRAIN YOUR BRAIN, CLIFF.

WE JUST HAVE TO WAIT FOR THEM TO FIGURE IT OUT, THEN GET TO LORAINE FIRST. WE'VE GOT THIS.

THEN WHAT ARE WE WAITING FOR? LET'S SNEAK UP AND SEE IF THEY GOT THE ANSWER YET.

YOU TWO COMING OR WHAT?

WE'RE GOING TO TRY USING OUR BRAINS INSTEAD.

PART OF A FAMILY, ALL GOING THE SAME WAY...

CARLY, THIS IS WRONG.

I WANT TO WIN FOR REAL, NOT BY CHEATING.

ME TOO.

BUT WHAT CAN WE DO?

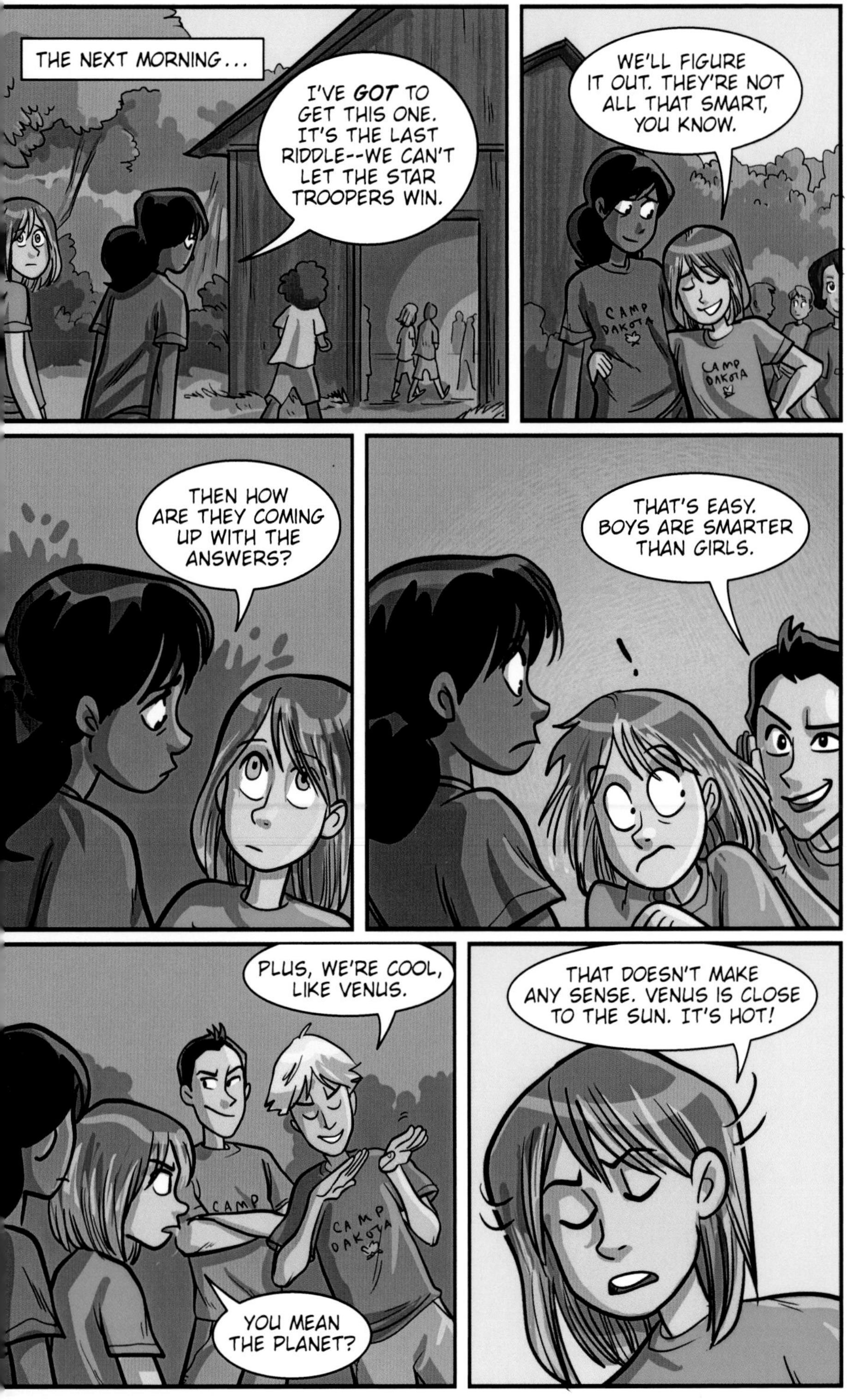
THE NEXT MORNING...
I'VE **GOT** TO GET THIS ONE. IT'S THE LAST RIDDLE--WE CAN'T LET THE STAR TROOPERS WIN.
WE'LL FIGURE IT OUT. THEY'RE NOT ALL THAT SMART, YOU KNOW.
CAMP DAKOTA
CAMP DAKOTA
THEN HOW ARE THEY COMING UP WITH THE ANSWERS?
THAT'S EASY. BOYS ARE SMARTER THAN GIRLS.
!
PLUS, WE'RE COOL, LIKE VENUS.
CAMP
CAMP DAKOTA
YOU MEAN THE PLANET?
THAT DOESN'T MAKE ANY SENSE. VENUS IS CLOSE TO THE SUN. IT'S HOT!

YEAH, RIGHT. HOW DO YOU KNOW?

WHAT ARE YOU BABBLING ABOUT?

MY VERY EXCELLENT MOTHER JUST SERVED US NACHOS.

IT'S HOW I REMEMBER THE ORDER OF THE PLANETS. MERCURY, VENUS, EARTH, MARS, JUPITER, SATURN, URANUS, NEPTUNE.

THERE'S AN OLD VERSION WITH A *P* WORD ON THE END, BUT THAT WAS BEFORE THEY DECIDED PLUTO WASN'T REALLY A PLANET.

WHATEVER. WEIRDOS.

IGNORE THEM. THAT'S PRETTY COOL, HOW YOU MEMORIZED THE ORDER OF THE PLANETS. I ONLY REMEMBER THAT THEY ALL ORBIT THE SUN!

OH MY GOSH! I THINK I KNOW THE ANSWER!

LORAINE!

LORAINE!

NO WAY, WE WERE HERE FIRST!

IT'S OK! WE DON'T HAVE THE ANSWER!

WE JUST NEED TO TALK TO LORAINE...ALONE.

WHAT IS GOING ON HERE?

YOU SEE, WELL, TEAM STAR TROOPERS IS KINDA...

CHEATING.

WHAT? HOW?

WE DIDN'T COME UP WITH THE ANSWERS OURSELVES.

LUKE AND CLIFF WERE EAVESDROPPING ON TEAM ASTRO EXPLORERS. THEN THEY RAN TO YOU WITH THE ANSWERS.

THIS IS PRETTY SERIOUS. YOU REALIZE WHAT THIS MEANS, DON'T YOU?

TEAM STAR TROOPERS IS DISQUALIFIED, ISN'T IT?

THAT'S RIGHT.

GOOD LUCK, YOU GUYS.

SO IT LOOKS LIKE YOUR TEAM IS IN THE LEAD NOW. WHAT DID YOU WANT TO SAY?

HUH? OH. THE THIRD RIDDLE... THE "FAMILY" IS THE PLANETS IN OUR SOLAR SYSTEM.

ALL OF THEM ORBIT THE SUN THE SAME WAY: COUNTERCLOCKWISE.

EACH PLANET SPINS ON ITS AXIS TOO.

MOST OF THEM SPIN COUNTERCLOCKWISE. BUT URANUS AND VENUS DO IT A LITTLE DIFFERENTLY.

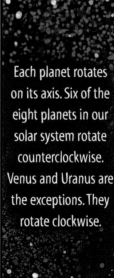

Each planet rotates on its axis. Six of the eight planets in our solar system rotate counterclockwise. Venus and Uranus are the exceptions. They rotate clockwise.

I THINK WE HAVE A WINNER.

TEAM ASTRO EXPLORERS HAS WON THE COMPETITION! THEY GET TO GO ON A SPECIAL ADVENTURE TO SEE THE BIG EVENT TOMORROW AFTERNOON.

DON'T WORRY, WE'LL ALL GET TO SEE IT. JUST NOT AS WELL AS TEAM ASTRO EXPLORERS WILL.

LORAINE? WHAT EXACTLY *IS* THE BIG EVENT?

IT'S A TOTAL SOLAR ECLIPSE!

A solar eclipse occurs when the Moon passes between the Sun and Earth, and the Moon blocks the Sun. In a total eclipse, the Moon blocks the Sun completely.

WHICH MEANS WE NEED TO MAKE SOME PINHOLE VIEWERS. TO THE ART CABIN, EVERYONE!

LOOKING DIRECTLY AT THE SUN CAN DAMAGE YOUR EYES, SO WE NEED A SAFE WAY TO LOOK AT THE ECLIPSE. WE'LL RECYCLE THESE CEREAL BOXES INTO PINHOLE VIEWERS.

FIRST, CUT OUT A PIECE OF WHITE PAPER THAT'S ABOUT THE SIZE OF THE BOTTOM OF YOUR BOX BUT A LITTLE SMALLER. THEN GLUE THAT PAPER TO THE BOTTOM INSIDE OF YOUR BOX.

NEXT, CUT OUT THE TOP OF YOUR BOX ON THE RIGHT AND LEFT SIDES AND CLOSE THE LID, SO IT LOOKS LIKE THIS.

THEN COVER ONE OF THOSE HOLES WITH FOIL AND TAPE IT DOWN.

LAST OF ALL, USE A NAIL TO MAKE A HOLE IN THE MIDDLE OF THE FOIL. DON'T MAKE IT VERY BIG!

TOMORROW WE'LL STAND WITH OUR BACKS TO THE SUN, SO THE SUN SHINES THROUGH THE HOLE IN THE FOIL.

WHEN YOU LOOK THROUGH THE OPEN CORNER, YOU'LL SEE AN IMAGE OF THE SUN ON THE WHITE PAPER INSIDE THE BOX.

KYLE? WE HEARD ABOUT WHAT CARLY AND BRAELIN DID...

WE WERE THINKING... MAYBE THEY COULD COME WITH US TOMORROW?

IT PROBABLY WASN'T EASY TO TELL THE TRUTH ABOUT THEIR TEAM. THEY SHOULD GET SOMETHING GOOD FOR DOING THAT.

AS LONG AS IT'S ALL RIGHT WITH YOUR TEAMMATES, I THINK THAT'S A FINE IDEA.

IF THE MOON AND EARTH HAD THE SAME TYPE OF ORBITS, WE'D SEE A TOTAL SOLAR ECLIPSE EVERY MONTH! BUT THEIR ORBITS ARE UNEVEN.

The Moon's orbit is slightly tilted, so Earth and the Moon line up to make a total solar eclipse about once every 18 months. The eclipse can only be seen from a small area on Earth each time.

AND SINCE THE SUN IS ABOUT 400 TIMES BIGGER THAN THE MOON BUT IS ALSO ABOUT 400 TIMES FARTHER AWAY, THEY BOTH LOOK AS IF THEY'RE THE SAME SIZE FROM HERE.

IS HE MAKING THOSE NUMBERS UP?

NO, HE'S NOT! IT'S TRUE.

OK, WE'RE HERE.

WE HAVE A FEW MINUTES. LET'S REST FOR A BIT.

ANYONE WANT SOME OF MY FAMOUS ULTRA-SUPER CHOCOLATE CHUNK COOKIES?

OH YEAH!

I'M SO EXCITED! I CAN'T BELIEVE I GET TO SEE A TOTAL ECLIPSE!

IT WON'T BE SCARY, WILL IT?

NO. BUT BEFORE PEOPLE UNDERSTOOD ABOUT ORBITS AND THINGS, ECLIPSES USED TO BE VERY SCARY.

YEAH, WHEN THE SKY GOT ALL DARK, PEOPLE THOUGHT THE MOON WAS EATING THE SUN AND THE WORLD WAS GOING TO END.

IT'S STARTING TO GET DARK NOW.

BUT NOW WE KNOW WHAT'S REALLY HAPPENING AND THAT THE SUN WILL COME OUT AGAIN JUST FINE.

LET'S GET OUT OUR VIEWERS. I THINK IT'S STARTING.

LOOK INTO THE BIG HOLE IN YOUR VIEWER, AND BE SURE TO FACE AWAY FROM THE SUN.

I CAN SEE THE SUN, AND IT DOESN'T HURT MY EYES. IT WORKS!

OK, HERE IT COMES! REMEMBER, DON'T LOOK DIRECTLY AT THE SUN.

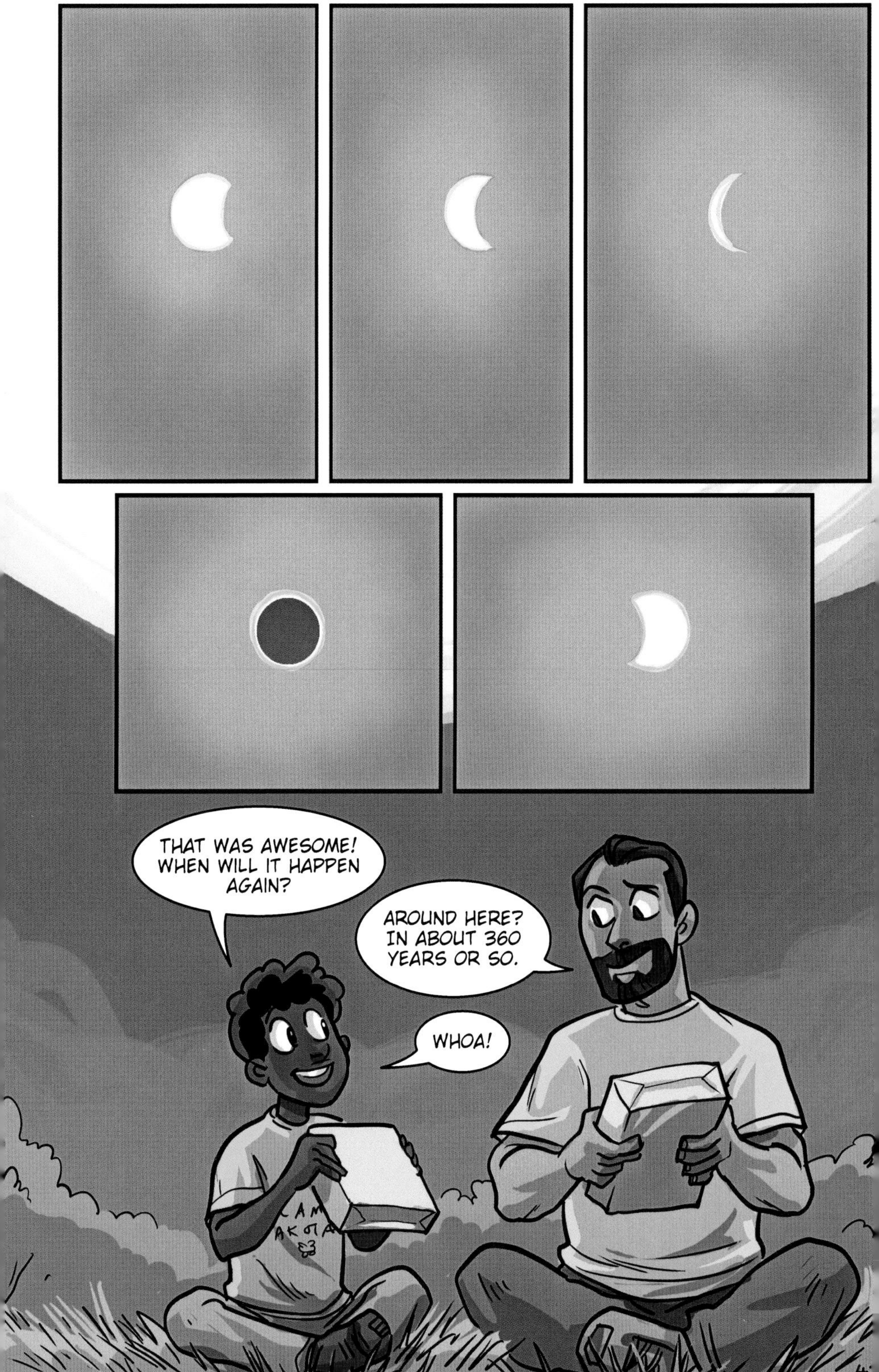
THAT WAS AWESOME! WHEN WILL IT HAPPEN AGAIN?
AROUND HERE? IN ABOUT 360 YEARS OR SO.
WHOA!

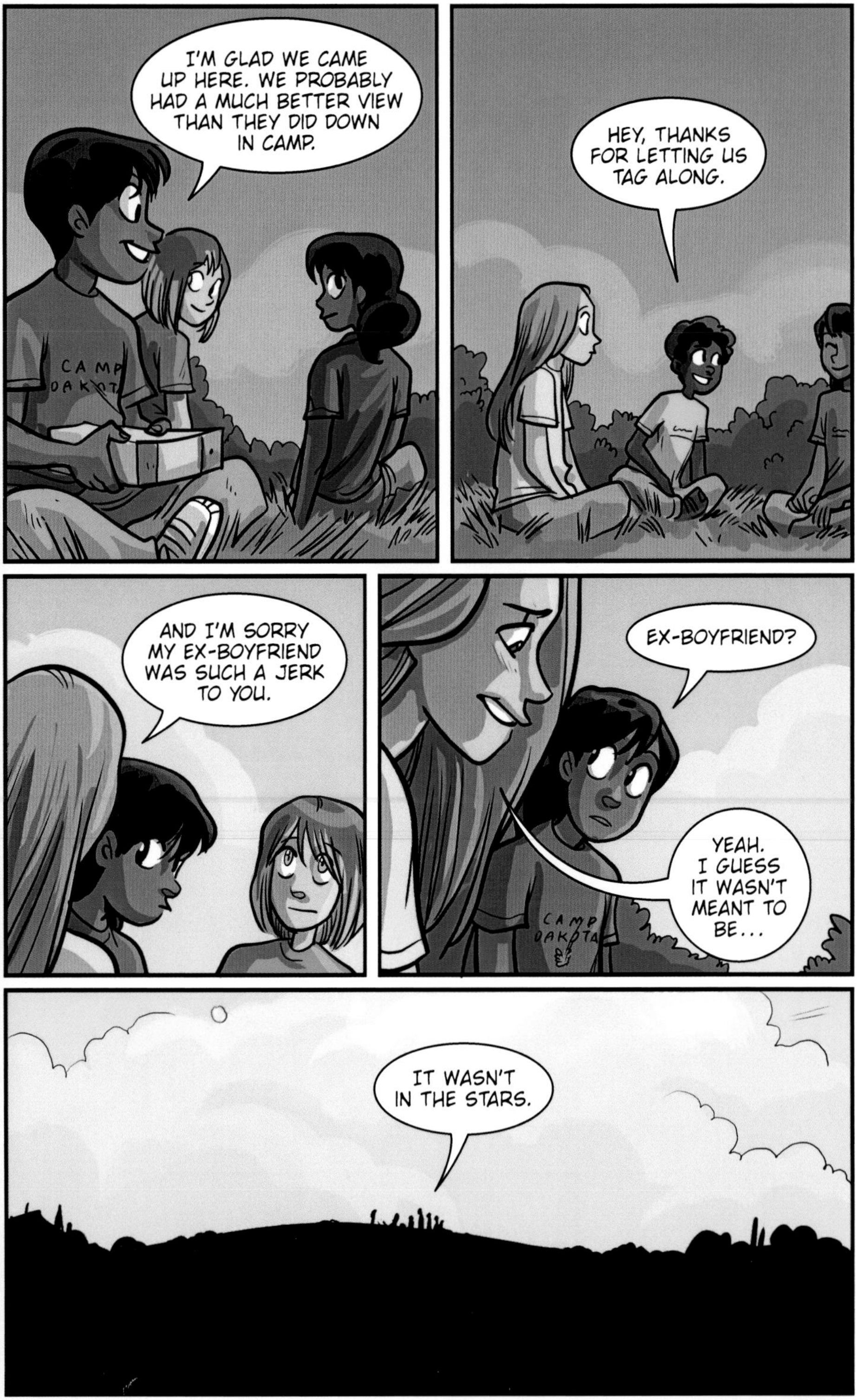
I'M GLAD WE CAME UP HERE. WE PROBABLY HAD A MUCH BETTER VIEW THAN THEY DID DOWN IN CAMP.
CAMP DAKOTA
HEY, THANKS FOR LETTING US TAG ALONG.
AND I'M SORRY MY EX-BOYFRIEND WAS SUCH A JERK TO YOU.
EX-BOYFRIEND?
YEAH. I GUESS IT WASN'T MEANT TO BE...
CAMP DAKOTA
IT WASN'T IN THE STARS.

***THE END***

# Experiments

Try these fun experiments at home or in your classroom.
Make sure you have an adult help you.

## Canned Planetarium

Don't have a planetarium near you? Don't worry, you can make your own.

You will need: a picture of a constellation; clean, empty tin cans; tracing paper; tape; nail; hammer; flashlight

1) Find a picture of a constellation, and use the tracing paper to make a copy of the star pattern. Make sure it is small enough to fit on the bottom of your can.

2) Flip the tracing paper over, and tape it to the bottom of a can. Your constellation should look backward.

3) Ask an adult to use the hammer to carefully pound the nail into the can wherever there is a dot on the tracing paper, just enough to make a small hole all the way through.

4) Take the tracing paper off your can. Turn out the lights, and shine your flashlight through the can, projecting the light onto your ceiling. The constellation will appear!

5) Repeat, using different cans, with as many different constellations as you like.

## What happened?

A planetarium is a place where people go to learn about astronomy. Images of the stars, planets, and other objects in the night sky are projected on a domed ceiling. By shining light through the holes in your tin can, you created your own planetarium. If your constellation looks backward, you forgot to flip the tracing paper over.

# Paper Plate Sundial

What you will need: paper plate, ruler, protractor, sharp pencil

1) Using the ruler, draw a straight line through the center of the paper plate. Then draw another straight line across the first one, so your lines divide the plate into four quarters.

2) Next, you will label your sundial, so you can tell what time it is. Where one line meets the end of the plate, write "12 PM." Rotate the sundial clockwise, and write "6 AM" on the next line. Rotate again, and write "12 AM." Rotate one more time and write "6 PM" on the last line.

3) Using the protractor, make a mark every 15 degrees between the lines. Then label each of these with the hours that are missing between what you already labeled.

4) Find a sunny spot outside that doesn't get shady all day long. Put your sundial down and poke your pencil through the center of it, pinning it to the ground. Make sure the pencil is standing up straight.

5) Check the time on your watch. Then rotate your sundial until the shadow from the pencil lands on the same time as your watch says.

## What happened?

As the Earth turns on its axis, the Sun appears to travel across the sky. This causes shadows to change length and position throughout the day. By observing these shadows we can tell time.

# Mysterious Words

**atmosphere:** the mass of gases surrounding a planet or star. Earth's atmosphere is known as air.

**axis:** an imaginary line around which a rotating object, such as Earth, turns

**comet:** a ball of ice, rock, and gases that travels around the Sun and develops a long, bright tail when it passes near the Sun

**constellation:** a group of stars that form a pattern and are given a name

**meteor:** a small piece of rock or metal that moves through the solar system

**solar eclipse:** an event when the Moon passes between Earth and the Sun, partly or completely blocking the Sun from view

**solar system:** the Sun and the group of bodies that rotate around it, including planets, moons, comets, meteoroids, and asteroids

**vaporize:** to change from a solid or a liquid into a gas

# Could YOU have solved the Great Space Case?

Good thing the kids of Camp Dakota knew a bit about astronomy—and got some helpful tips from the counselors. See if you caught all the facts they put to use.

- Comets are sometimes called dirty snowballs because they are made of ice, dust, and rocks. If a comet is moving toward the Sun, a tail is formed behind it. If the comet is moving away from the Sun, the tail is in front.

- A meteoroid is a small chunk of rock or metal that moves through the solar system. When it enters Earth's atmosphere its surface begins to burn. This creates a bright streak in the sky called a meteor. If a meteor lands on Earth, it's called a meteorite.

- There are eight planets in the solar system. For a long time Pluto was considered the ninth planet, but now scientists know that it's too small to be a true planet. All the planets orbit the Sun counterclockwise, and each rotates on its axis the same way, with two exceptions: Venus and Uranus.

# THE AUTHOR

**LYNDA BEAUREGARD** wrote her first story when she was seven years old and hasn't stopped writing since. She also likes teaching kids how to swim; designing websites; directing race cars out onto the track; and throwing bouncy balls for her cat, Becca. She lives near Detroit, Michigan, with her two lovely daughters, who are doing their best to turn her hair gray.

# THE ARTIST

**DER-SHING HELMER** graduated from the University of California—Berkeley, where she played with snakes and lizards all summer long. When she is not teaching biology to high school students, she is making art and comics for everyone to enjoy. Her best friends are her two pet geckos (Smeg and Jerry), her king snake (Clarice), and the chinchilla that lives next door.